For:
With love:
Charlie's
AUTO REPAIR
123
SESAME STREET
123

by Sesame Workshop
Illustrated by Ernie Kwiat

LOVE is a

Sunny
DAY!

# LOVE is

dancing by yourself to your favorite song.

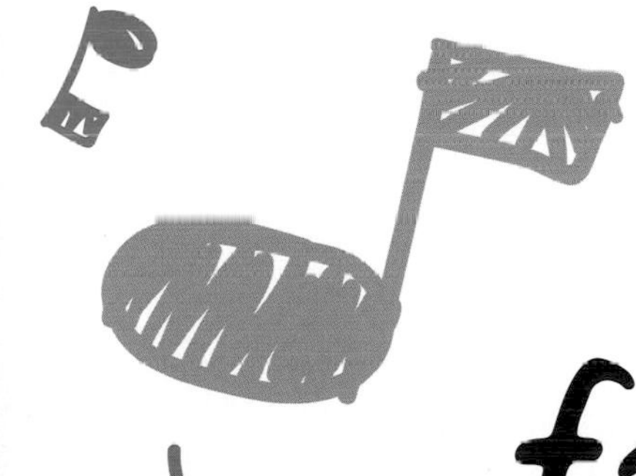

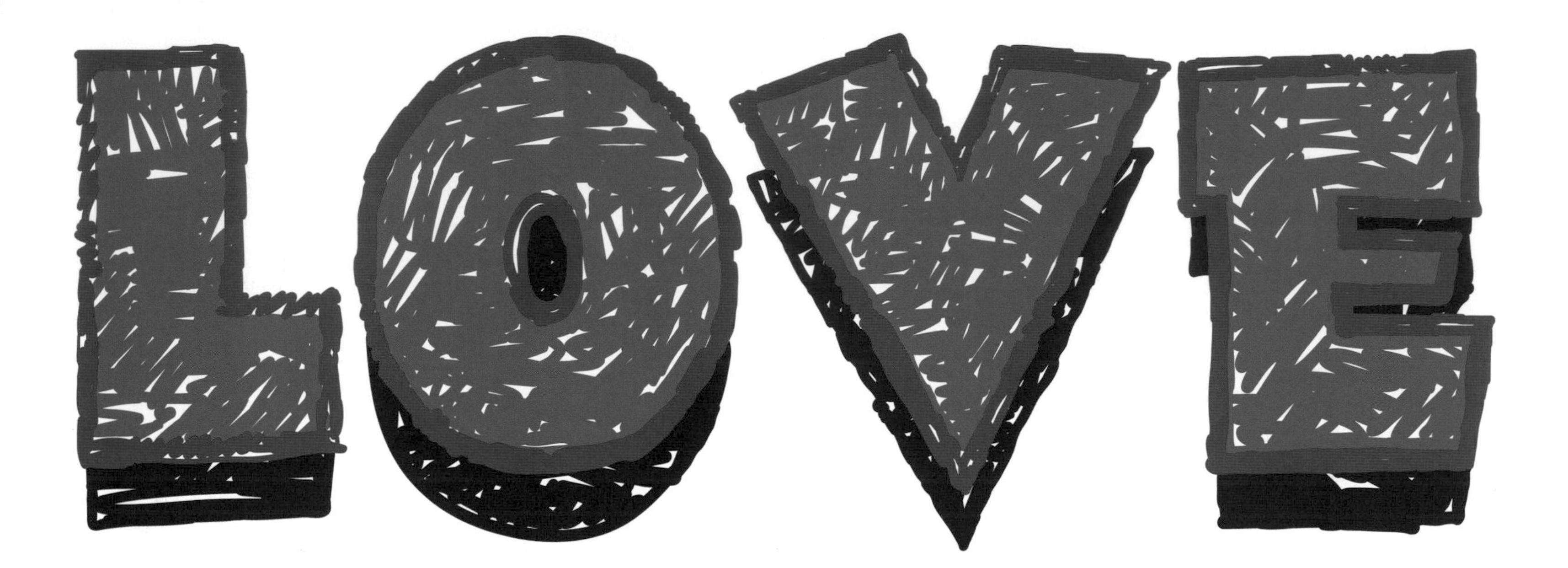


IS BEING AN EVERYDAY

AH, AH,
AH!

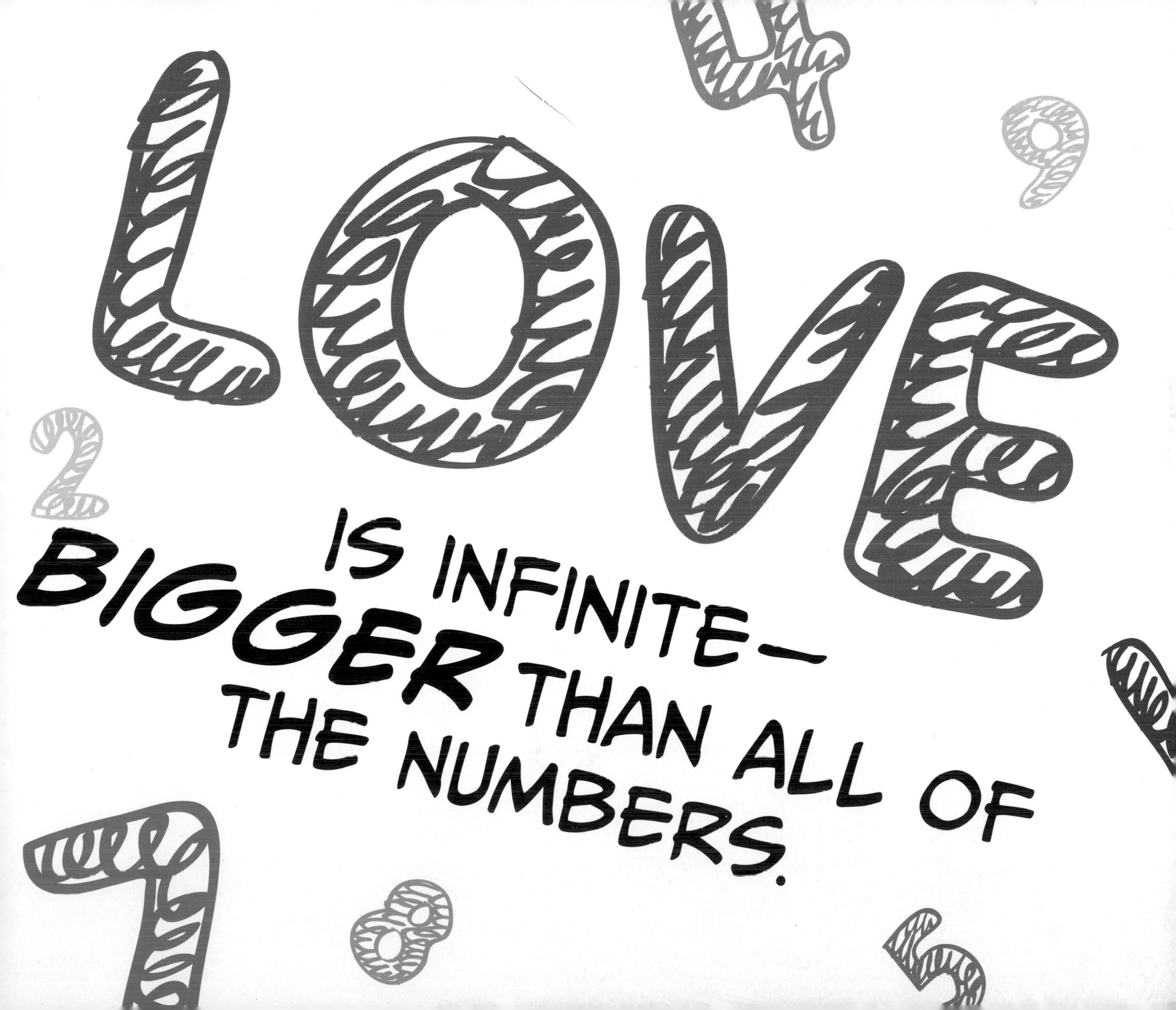
LOVE
IS INFINITE—
BIGGER THAN ALL OF
THE NUMBERS.

comes in all

SHAPES and SIZEs.

LOVE

is
building
something
together.

IS GIGGLES,
AND KISSES, AND HUGS,
AND SQUISHES.

SINGS IN
EVERY LANGUAGE.

LA LA LA

LA LA LA

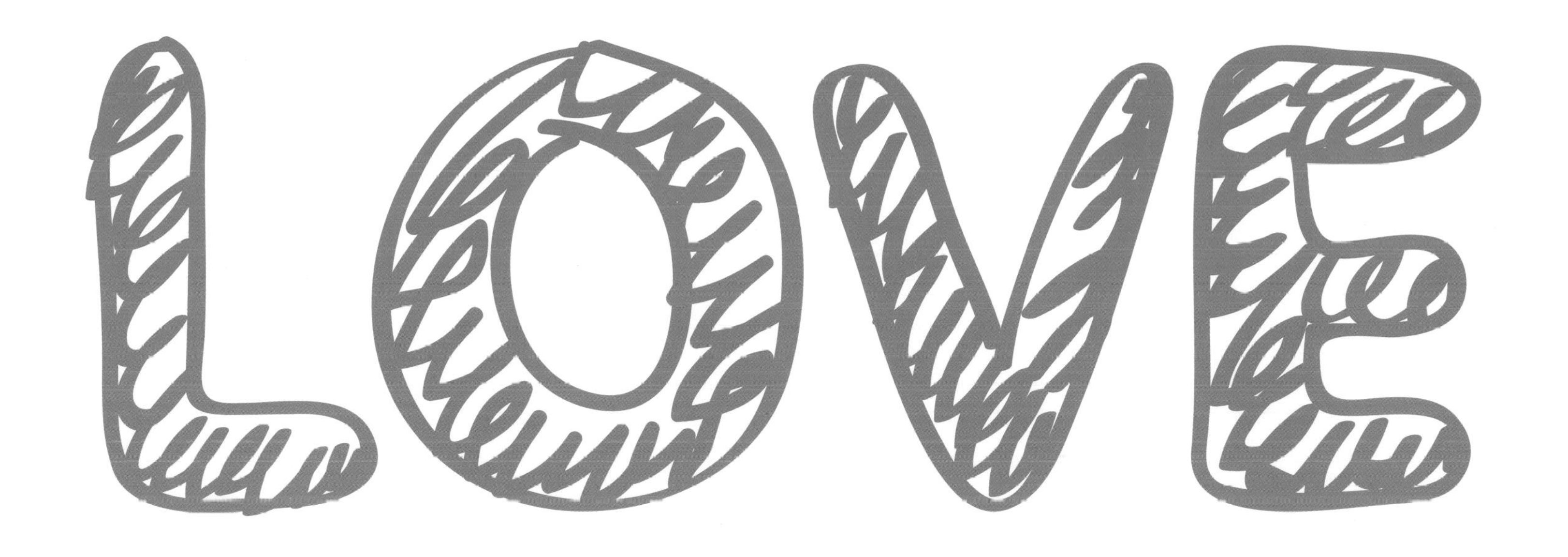


is being kind to all your best friends.

LOVE

MAKES ALL KINDS OF SOUNDS.

HONK, HONK!

I LIKE IT MESSY.
SODA

LOVE
IS ACCEPTING
LIFE EVEN WHEN
IT IS MESSY!

AMAZING FAMILY

and a soft bunny.

Love

is
Cookies...
and then
more cookies.

LOVE is magical and full of WONDER.

Love is everywhere

and all around us.

Text by Craig Manning
Illustrations by Ernie Kwiat



Published by Sourcebooks Jabberwocky, an imprint of Sourcebooks, Inc.
P.O. Box 4410, Naperville, Illinois 60567-4410
(630) 961-3900
Fax: (630) 961-2168
sourcebooks.com

Source of Production: 1010 Printing International,
North Point, Hong Kong, China
Date of Production: November 2018
Run Number: 5013822

Printed and bound in China.
OGP 10 9 8 7 6 5 4 3 2

Mama's
CAFE
BUS STOP
OPEN
LAUNDROMAT
HOOPER'S STORE